P9-BIW-913

Hunter & Stripe
and the
Soccer
Showdown

By Laura Malone Elliott

Illustrations by Lynn Munsinger

KATHERINE TEGEN BOOKS
An Imprint of HarperCollins Publishers

To John and Gene and coaches like
them who foster team camaraderie,
fair play, respect for opponents, and
FUN.
–L.M.E.

For Alex, Kendall, and Lara
–L.M.

Hunter and Stripe and the Soccer Showdown
Text copyright © 2005 by Laura Malone Elliott
Illustrations copyright © 2005 by Lynn Munsinger
Manufactured in China.
www.harperchildrens.com
Library of Congress Cataloging-in-Publication Data is available.
ISBN 0-06-052759-5 — ISBN 0-06-052760-9 (lib. bdg.)

Typography by Al Cetta   1 2 3 4 5 6 7 8 9 10   ❖   First Edition

Hunter and Stripe were best friends.

They helped each other learn to read,

to shoot a basketball,

to make eights that looked like snowmen,

and to sing "The Star-Spangled Banner."

At Halloween, they both
dressed as Robin Raccoonhood.

They even liked the same girl: Rowena Rebecca Rachel.

Hunter and Stripe did everything together. Until soccer—somehow, they ended up on different teams.

"That's okay," Hunter's dad told him. "You'll *play* Stripe's team."

Hunter's dad volunteered to coach Hunter's team, the Comets.
Stripe's father coached Stripe's team, the Sharks.

During practices, Hunter and Stripe learned to dribble, to pass the ball to teammates, and to slam it into the goal.

Hunter was really fast. He could break away and race the ball down the field.

Stripe had terrific foot control. He could dance the ball around his opponents.

Both of them scored a lot. Both were undefeated.

One weekend, Hunter watched Stripe's team play.
Stripe's mom had made a shark flag with pointy teeth and a
huge fin. Stripe and his teammates put their paws on top of
their heads like fins, and sang:

"Sharks, sharks, get a score.

Steal the ball and make more, more, more!"

Stripe scored the first and last goal. Hunter cheered.
Stripe's team won, 5 to 3.

The next Saturday, Stripe came to Hunter's game.
Hunter's mom had made a flag, too. She'd sewn a big
red ball with yellow flames shooting out the back. Sticking
their tails straight out like comets, Hunter's team shouted,
"Yaaaaaaaaay, Comets!"

Hunter scored three goals. Stripe cheered. Hunter's team won, 6 to 5.

On Monday, trouble started.

"We play you Saturday," said Stripe. "We've never been beaten." He put his paw on Hunter's shoulder and said, "So don't feel bad when you lose."

Hunter shook off his best friend's paw. "Why would I lose?"

Stripe frowned. "Because I can dribble circles around you."

"Well, I can outrun you."

"Oh, yeah?" said Stripe. "Race you to the swings. On your mark . . . get set . . ." Stripe darted away and then shouted, "GO!" over his shoulder.

Hunter ran to catch up, but Stripe reached the swings first.

"You cheated," Hunter cried.

"Did not," Stripe shouted.

They stomped away in opposite directions. They didn't play together all week long.

The day of the soccer showdown arrived. It was the last game of the season. Since both teams were undefeated, whichever team won would be the league champs.

Being mad at Stripe only made Hunter want to beat the Sharks more. But he also was embarrassed that he hoped Stripe would mess up. He picked at his breakfast.

His big sister, Glenna, said, "Don't worry. I only hated Cleo for two months after she beat me in the tennis tournament."

"What?!"

"Just kidding. It was only two weeks. Here's what my coach says: 'It's a game. It should be fun. It's even more fun when the other team is good. That's when you play your best. Sports should celebrate the amazing things we can do—no matter who wins.'"

"Huh?"

Glenna smiled mysteriously. "You'll see."

When the Comets and the Sharks ran onto the field,
their parents shook signs at each other and shouted:
"Yaaaay, Comets" and "Sharks, Sharks, Sharks!"

Hunter played center forward. So did Stripe. They lined up, whisker to whisker.

"Prepare to lose, bottlenose," snarled Stripe.

"Prepare yourself, bush-tail," Hunter sniped back.

Hunter got his foot on the ball first. Like lightning, he skittered it down the field, the Sharks chasing him like crazy. Hunter slammed the ball into the goal.

Wow, thought Stripe. Pretty good. But he didn't say anything.

Stripe's team got the ball. Stripe tapped the ball left, knocked it right, popped it with the outside of his foot, and nudged it with the inside. The Comet players were getting dizzy. Hunter turned around like a corkscrew. Stripe scored. Wow, thought Hunter. But he didn't say anything either.

And so the game went, until there were only five minutes left. The score was tied, 3 to 3.

That's when the coaches got a little crazy.

"Paw-ball!" Hunter's dad yelled when the ball bounced up off the ground and caught Stripe's thumb.

"Out of bounds!" Stripe's dad screamed when Hunter took the ball down the sideline, his little toe just touching the edge.

Hunter's dad jumped onto the field to discuss the call
with the referee. So did Stripe's.

"That was in!" Hunter's dad yelled.

"Was not!" shouted Stripe's dad.

Hunter's dad and Stripe's dad got snout to snout and started wagging their fingers at each other. They talked so fast and so loud, neither of them made any sense. Even the ref looked confused.

Hunter and Stripe started to giggle. "Your dad sounds like Glenna's Rappin' Raccoon doll when it gets stuck on high," said Hunter.

"Your dad sounds like he's on fast forward," said Stripe.

Hunter and Stripe had to cover their mouths, they were laughing so hard.

It felt great to be sharing a joke again.

"Hey, Stripe. Good game," said Hunter.

"You too, Hunter."

"Let's go, guys," called the ref.

This time when they lined up, Hunter and Stripe grinned at each other.

Hunter nabbed the ball and tore down the field. He launched it with a beautiful kick. It sailed for the goal, and . . . Stripe trapped it!

Stripe waltzed the ball around one Comet after another. He crossed it downfield to another Shark, who whacked it into the goal just as the ref blew his whistle to end the game.

The Sharks won, 4 to 3.

For a long time, Hunter just stood there. He felt awful.
He had so wanted to be champ. He struggled to be a good
sport, his best self. Stripe's team had played great. So had
Hunter's. Now Hunter knew what Glenna meant. When
both teams pushed to play their absolute best, the game was
more exciting.

Stripe saw Hunter looking so sad and beaten. He
stopped jumping up and down. "You sure are fast, Hunter."

Hunter took a deep breath. If he had to lose, he was
glad his friend could win.

"Thanks, Stripe. Congratulations."

Hunter and Stripe rode home together. Stripe said, "I'll race you to our tree house."

Together, they recited, "On your mark . . . get set . . . GO!"

Off they darted, neck and neck. When they reached the tree, they fell onto the grass, laughing.

That afternoon, anyway, Hunter didn't even notice that he got there first.